Tadpoles

Mop Top

First published in 2006 by
Franklin Watts
338 Euston Road
London
NW1 3BH

Franklin Watts Australia
Hachette Children's Books
Level 17/207 Kent Street
Sydney
NSW 2000

A CIP catalogue record for this book is available
from the British Library.

ISBN (10) 0 7496 6545 9 (hbk)
ISBN (13) 978-0-7496-6545-6 (hbk)
ISBN (10) 0 7496 6895 4 (pbk)
ISBN (13) 978-0-7496-6895-2 (pbk)

Series Editor: Jackie Hamley
Series Advisor: Dr Hilary Minns
Series Designer: Peter Scoulding

Printed in China

Mop Top

by Sue Graves

Illustrated by Maddy McClellan

W
FRANKLIN WATTS
LONDON•SYDNEY

Sue Graves

"I don't have a dog, but I do have a cat. Luckily, I don't have to worry about keeping the hair out of her eyes, unlike poor Henry with Mop Top."

Maddy McClellan

"I had a dog called Skipper when I was Henry's age. I got him for my birthday and I was SO excited that I ignored all my friends!"

Henry's puppy had
a shaggy coat.

He was so shaggy
that everyone called
him Mop Top!

But Mop Top's coat
grew ...

... and grew!

Mum tied it up
into bunches.

But that was no good.

13

Dad gave Mop Top
his cap.

But that was no good.

Then Henry had an idea. He told Mum.

They went to
see Annie.

Annie gave Mop Top
a haircut.

"Now Mop Top is a crop top!" laughed Henry.

Notes for adults

TADPOLES is structured to provide support for newly independent read
The stories may also be used by adults for sharing with young children

Starting to read alone can be daunting. **TADPOLES** helps by providir
visual support and repeating words and phrases. These books will both
develop confidence and encourage reading and rereading for pleasure

If you are reading this book with a child, here are a few suggestions:

1. Make reading fun! Choose a time to read when you and the child are
relaxed and have time to share the story.

2. Talk about the story before you start reading. Look at the cover and
the blurb. What might the story be about? Why might the child like it?

3. Encourage the child to reread the story, and to retell the story in their
own words, using the illustrations to remind them what has happened.

4. Discuss the story and see if the child can relate it to their own experien
or perhaps compare it to another story they know.

5. Give praise! Remember that small mistakes need not always be correct

If you enjoyed this book, why not try

another **TADPOLES** story?